FRED
TO THE RESCUE

The Adventures of Fred
Published by Fawcett Columbine

FRED TO THE RESCUE
FRED IN CHARGE
FRED AND THE PET SHOW PANIC
FRED SAVES THE DAY

FRED
TO THE RESCUE

by Leslie McGuire

Illustrated by Dave Henderson

Fawcett Columbine • New York

CONTENTS

CHAPTER ONE

BLACK MONDAY

It was a very bad day. It started out as a bad day and then it got worse. In fact, last Monday was the worst day I have ever had.

It's partly because I saved Mr. Duff. Then *he* had the nerve to say he didn't need saving. What does he know? He was too close to the road, and a car was coming. So I knocked him into a bush. He said he was on the sidewalk, right where he belonged. He said the car was in the street, right where it belonged.

I say, so what? I saved his life, but did he thank me? No. He called me a fathead! I've seen some very nutty drivers lately. You never know what a car is going to do. Safe

is safe, right? But that's not what Mr. Duff said.

What's more, last Monday was Halloween. You may think Halloween is fun. I don't. For one thing, you can't tell the good guys from the bad guys. Not only that, you can't tell who needs saving and who doesn't. Even the good guys are being bad.

But first, let me explain. I am Fred. I am the Duff family dog. The Duffs are sweet, but they are not too smart. They are very careless. It's my job to keep them safe. They do not make my job easy.

I'm a Saint Bernard. It is a Saint Bernard's solemn duty to save people. They've been saving people for centuries. They are very good at it. So am I.

Saint Bernards are the dogs that carry little barrels of brandy under their chins. They save people stuck in the snow or lost in the woods. The people they save are supposed to drink the brandy to make them strong.

That is silly. I think chicken soup would work much better. After all, brandy tastes disgusting. But on the other hand, cold chicken soup also tastes disgusting.

The difference between most Saint Bernards and me is that most Saint Bernards don't have to live in a house full of clumsy people. Unfortunately, I do.

The Duffs are always getting into trouble. Especially Arnie. So are all of Arnie's little friends. Arnie is ten, but the most important thing about Arnie is that I am his dog. I have to keep my eye on all of the Duffs all of the time.

The Duffs and me—Fred—live in a small town called Big Bluff. Big Bluff has a small harbor with boats, and (you guessed it) a big bluff. A bluff is like a cliff. This cliff is about two hundred feet high. The Duff house is right on top of the bluff. Sometimes the Duffs call it Duff's Bluff.

Personally, I find the bluff a problem. I spend a good part of my day making sure nobody falls off the bluff. If Arnie isn't getting too close, Mr. Duff or someone else is.

There are only four Duffs (not counting me). But sometimes it feels as if there are hundreds of them.

Mr. Duff says I'm the problem. He's wrong. What is more important? Getting the lawn mowed or staying alive? Safe is safe, I always say.

Sometimes they try to lock me up. This never works. I am the Houdini of Dogs. In case you didn't know, Houdini was a great escape artist. He could get out of anything. He could get out of a locked wooden box with chains all around it while he was wearing a blindfold and a straitjacket with the sleeves tied behind his back. I can get out of anything, too. I always get out just in the nick of time. Each time they lock me up, I end up saving them all from something.

I have a dog door all my own. But there is a sliding panel which is sometimes shut. This doesn't matter. I have ways of getting out anyhow. But I won't tell my secrets. Let's just say that part of being the Houdini of Dogs is being prepared for the worst.

Well, maybe I'll tell you one secret. I found a small block of wood and stuck it on the jamb of the side door. That way, it doesn't close all the way.

Anyhow, saving Mr. Duff and getting called a fathead was just the beginning. That was the *good* part of the day. The bad part was next.

But I was prepared.

CHAPTER TWO

WHY ME? WHY NOT?

So, after being called a fathead—and in front of two cats and Winston—I went inside the house. Winston is a ridiculous excuse for a dog. He lives next door.

Winston was sniggering. That is why I went inside. Winston's sniggering is a horrible noise. It sounds like a clogged drain. Winston makes that noise when he laughs because he's a pug. His nose looks as if he's just crashed into a door.

When I got inside, I noticed that it was too quiet in the house. This always means trouble. But I couldn't check into it right away. I was too upset and needed a magazine. I found two copies of *Field and Stream* plus a copy of *Seventeen* on the coffee table. The *Field and Stream* was tasty as ever. The *Seventeen* tasted terrible. It's because of all those perfume ads. Yech.

But I didn't care what it tasted like. I was a mess. I had a very bad feeling about what was coming next. It was going to be a long night, so I binged. That means I ate way too much. I learned about binging from an article on eating problems. I read it last month while I was eating a copy of *People* magazine. It was about movie stars. Eating too much is a problem I can understand.

I had just gotten to a very interesting but terrible-tasting part in *Seventeen.* It was a quiz. "Is Your Boyfriend Right for You?" Then Arnie came home.

Arnie is the smallest Duff and my biggest problem. I can't figure out how anyone so small can get into so much trouble. I am taller than Arnie when I'm sitting down and he's standing up, and I *never* get into trouble.

But size is not the problem here. The problem seems to be that Arnie can see.

8

Arnie wears glasses. But he didn't always. This is the first year that Arnie has ever really *seen* anything. No one knew he was near-sighted until last summer. When they figured it out, Arnie got glasses. Now he's seeing everything for the first time.

You would think that being able to see would help. But it doesn't. It makes things worse. Arnie sees little tiny things. He sees things that are far away. He even sees weird things. Arnie can see everything—except where he's going. And Arnie is always running off to get a better look at something.

So he trips a lot. So I have to save him a lot. It's very tiring.

Anyway, when Arnie came in, he didn't even stop to pet me. He ran right up the stairs to his room. I went back to my magazine. I always read while I eat. I like to keep up with the latest news. The quiz was very interesting, and I decided that Katie should read it.

Katie is Arnie's big sister. She isn't clumsy, but her boyfriend, Pete, is ridiculous. Katie

is a teenager, but she isn't too bad. That's because her hairdo is good. Not that I know
a lot about hairstyles, but her hair looks a lot
like mine. It's kind of long and shaggy.

Anyway, I thought if she read the article, she might think about Pete. Maybe she'd bring someone home who wouldn't bang into furniture all the time.

I was just about to go find Katie when two things happened at once. First, a huge, furry thing with pointy ears, a long, ratlike tail, and whiskers ran by. I started to growl. Then I realized it was Katie.

Great Jumping Fire Hydrants! She was dressed as a cat! What a totally mean thing to do! That really hurt my feelings!

I was about to let Katie know how I felt about her Halloween costume when the second thing happened. Katie started to scream.

CHAPTER THREE

NO JUSTICE!

This is what happens when Katie screams. Mirrors shatter and glasses break. Well, not really. But for a dog, it's very painful. Especially if you're in the same room. We dogs have very delicate ears, you know.

"How could you?" she screeched. "It's the new one! I didn't even get a chance to read it yet!"

Then she went down and ripped the magazine out of my mouth. Of course, she tore the quiz I wanted to show her.

The rest of the Duffs came running in to see why Katie was howling. Then, as luck would have it, the doorbell started to ring.

"Ma! He *drooled* all over it!" she yelled,

while waving what was left of *Seventeen* in my face. "Gross!"

Mrs. Duff went to answer the door. She doesn't like getting in the middle of family fights. Mrs. Duff is big and round and sweet. But she forgets things a lot. Aside from that, Mrs. Duff is actually the most careful of the Duffs. She has only one really weak area, and I don't mind that one.

You see, Mrs. Duff forgets to put food away. This is dangerous, because food that has been left out on the kitchen table can go bad. So I *have* to eat it. Right? I wouldn't want anyone to get sick from eating bad food, would I? As you can see, I am a very thoughtful dog.

Anyway, Katie was yelling, the doorbell was ringing, and Mrs. Duff was answering the door. Then Mr. Duff stomped in to find out what all the fuss was about. Mr. Duff is big, and bald. Even though he acts kind of grumpy, he's really a nice guy.

Mr. Duff also wears glasses. I think people who wear glasses can't see—with or without their glasses. I have to save Mr. Duff all the time.

Mr. Duff's glasses were a mess. There were twigs and leaves sticking in them. That must have been from the bush I knocked him into. Mr. Duff rolled his eyes at the ceiling and then stomped upstairs. He muttered something about how he should have stayed at work, where he was safe from me. Mrs. Duff heard the remark when she came back.

"I was thinking of getting a job, too," she said.

That one surprised me.

"Good idea," said Mr. Duff from the top of the stairs. "It's the only place where a person doesn't need to get rescued all the time."

Since I've never been to his job, I'm not sure about how safe it really is. But if Mr. Duff thinks it's safe, then it probably isn't.

"I think Fred should get a job," Katie said.

"Doing what?" asked Mr. Duff. "And where?"

"How about in a nursery school making little kids line up?" Katie said as she stamped into the kitchen. "This family could use some peace—and a lot less dog drool!"

Talk about ungrateful. Not one of them would be alive today if it weren't for me. That's a fact.

Then the kitchen door banged shut. I turned to get a good look at who was behind Mrs. Duff.

It was Beth Woods and Mike Peese. They are friends of Arnie's. Of course, they didn't look anything like the real Beth Woods and Mike Peese.

Beth looked like a big pumpkin, and Mike was covered with parts of his bed. I guessed he was supposed to be a ghost and that's why he was covered with sheets. The only way I knew who they were was because Beth smelled like Beth, and Mike was wearing his camera over all the bedding. Mike never goes anyplace without his camera.

Mike is Arnie's best friend. He likes to take pictures of things. The Duff house is one of Mike's favorite places to hang out. Mike says neat things are always happening—like me saving people. He has pictures of me saving everyone. Living proof. No one likes those pictures very much. I don't know why not. I do.

I like Mike a lot. I hope one of his pictures gets on the front page of the *Big Bluff News*. Then I'll be famous. I deserve to be famous. Maybe I should get ahold of one of those pictures and drop it off at the newspaper office. I'm sure they're looking for something really good to print. I read that paper a lot. Most of what's in there isn't worth the twenty-five cents they charge for it.

There was a clatter on the stairs. That's when I smelled something very odd. I looked up and saw a greenish, blackish, grayish, gloppy thing. It was wearing glasses. It smelled like melted plastic. It had to be Arnie.

"Gross," said Beth.

"That costume is the pits," said Katie, who had just come out of the kitchen again.

"Awesome," said Mike.

"Fred ith the greatetht dog in the uni-

17

verth," Arnie said proudly. He gave me a pat on the head.

"He certainly is, dear," said Mrs. Duff. "But what are you?"

"I am the Living Dead!"

He had a white thing in his mouth. Whatever it was made it hard for him to talk. Whatever it was looked like fangs.

"No you're not," said Katie. "You're just disgusting."

The white thing fell out of Arnie's mouth just in time.

"I mean, where would we all be without Fred?" Arnie said, pushing his glasses back up his nose. There was gray-green glop on the bottoms of the rims. "Without Fred, none of us would be alive today!"

That boy may be little and clumsy, but he's smart.

Arnie started to tell everyone about some of my more daring rescues.

"Remember the time Fred saved us all from—" he said.

But he didn't get to finish the sentence.

Suddenly Beth started to squeak and giggle and wiggle all over the place.

"What's wrong, dear?" asked Mrs. Duff.

"It's Mary Lou!" Beth said with a shriek. She reached into her pumpkin. "She got loose! She's running all around!"

CHAPTER FOUR

YOU REALLY KNOW HOW TO HURT A DOG

You are probably wondering who Mary Lou is. That is a perfectly normal thing to wonder. Mary Lou is Beth's pet frog. That's right. You heard me. A frog. I like Beth. But sometimes she can be very strange.

You see, Beth also rescues things. But she rescues animals. The big difference between the two of us is that the animals Beth rescues don't *need* rescuing. The people I rescue definitely do need rescuing. But she tries hard.

Beth's father is a scientist. He collects things like spiders and snakes and frogs. Beth thinks the spiders and snakes and frogs are sweet. I'm not too sure about the spiders and the snakes. The frogs are okay. They are just boring.

Beth lives in a big house. She has no brothers or sisters. But she has lots and lots of pets. Mostly they are animals she has rescued. They would probably like to be back in the woods.

Mary Lou is Beth's favorite frog. Beth takes Mary Lou everywhere. I think trick-or-treating with a frog is a mistake. But Beth claims that Mary Lou likes to travel. Maybe some trick-or-treating will make Mary Lou less boring. I doubt it.

It took Beth about five minutes to catch Mary Lou inside the pumpkin costume. She finally got Mary Lou back into her little plastic carrier. Then Arnie got back to his great story about some of my more daring rescues. He picked my favorite. It was the time when I saved all of them from a forest fire.

"That was no forest fire," Katie said with a sniff.

"He was worried," said Mrs. Duff. She smiled at me.

"Worried!" said Katie. "That was our cookout, and Fred wrecked it!"

This was not true. That campfire was about to set the whole woods on fire. Katie has a very bad memory. Besides, safe is safe.

"What about the time Fred saved you from falling off the big slide?" Arnie went on.

"I wasn't falling," she said. "I was sliding. That's what you're *supposed* to do on a slide."

"I've got pictures of lots of Fred's great rescues," Mike said from under all the sheets. "That's why I've got my camera tonight. I bet I'll get even more great rescue shots!"

Then Mike giggled. Beth and Arnie and Katie looked gloomy. I have no idea why. It was a great idea.

In fact, I could see the newspaper headline right before my eyes.

DOG BRAVES MONSTER! SAVES TOWN!

What a great way to hit the front page! I was lying there on the rug dreaming about the parade in my honor. And the big party! And the statue in front of town hall!

Just as I was dreaming about making my speech, Arnie whipped out a weird-looking gray thing with wires. He stuck it on my head.

Katie and Beth started making cooing noises. They sounded like sick birds.

"Ooooh!" they said. "How cu-u-ute!"

I knew something was very, very wrong.

"What a great idea!" Mrs. Duff said. "Fred's got a costume, too! A mouse! How clever!"

Clever, my foot. Arnie had put mouse ears on me!

Well, I guess I don't have to tell you how very upsetting that was. I shook my head. I tried to shake the mouse ears loose. I thought I could end this whole mouse business right then and there. But the ears would not come off.

Already my daydream was turning into a

nightmare. There was no way I could save the town from monsters and then get my picture on the front page of the newspaper wearing mouse ears! After all, I have a repu-

24

tation to keep up in this town! I have worked very hard on it. Mouse ears aren't part of it.

I wedged myself between the couch and the wall. I tried to rub the ears off. They didn't budge.

I started rolling around on the floor, twisting and bumping. No good. Those things were stuck!

Arnie tried to make me sit still. I slipped right through his hands. The trouble was, by this time, Arnie's hands were coated with the grease he'd put all over his face.

I rolled around so much, I knocked over the lamp. Arnie put it back up and got grease all over the shade. Soon I was completely covered with grease. I could feel my fur sticking up in little spikes all over my neck and down my back.

There was no way I was setting foot out of the house until those ridiculous things were off my head. But sadly, duty called.

Before I could do anything about it, the kids had gotten their bags, and were heading

out the front door. I had no choice but to fol-
low them.

On the way out the door, I saw myself in
the big hall mirror. I looked like a vampire
bat.

Oh well, I thought. Tonight is going to be
a waste anyway. I tried to cheer myself up.
I hoped maybe I would be able to lose the
ears somewhere along the way.

I raced out after Beth and Arnie and
Katie. It was cold, and dark. The air was
filled with strange giggling sounds.

My teeth were starting to grind.

CHAPTER FIVE

THE SHAME OF IT ALL

As soon as I set foot outside, Winston started gurgling again. It was the old clogged drain himself.

"It's the real you," Winston snuffled. "I love it."

"Blow it out your nose," I said cheerfully.

Winston can be a good pal sometimes. But there are other times when he gets on my nerves. Tonight was one of those times.

The two cats were sitting on the fence. Their names are Sam and Janet. They belong to Mr. and Mrs. Evening. They are called Sam and Janet Evening.

If you say their names together real fast, it sounds like you're saying "Some En-

27

chanted Evening." That's the title of a song. I heard it on television once. Can you believe it? I guess the Evenings think that's pretty funny.

Anyway, Sam and Janet are Siamese cats, and they have awful whiny voices. When they talk, it sounds like fingernails going across blackboards.

"We wouldn't go out looking like that," they said together. They always talk together. That doubles the pain. "A cat might get you!"

I took a few steps toward them. I enjoy scaring cats. I do it whenever I get the chance. Sam and Janet hopped off the fence, and landed on a tree branch.

"I wouldn't go out at all if I were you," I said.

Winston giggled. "Want me to come along and protect you, Fred?" he asked.

"Thanks, but no thanks," I said. "Gotta run."

The kids were almost at the end of the block. The light was red. I knew I had to catch up just in case they decided to cross anyway. Safe is safe.

I got there just in time. Katie was putting her foot off the curb. I threw myself in front of her. She started to fall.

"Oh, Fred!" she said. "Stop worrying so much!"

"He worries because he loves you," said Beth.

"Well," Katie snapped. "I love him, too. But I don't worry about him all the time, do I?"

That's because you don't have to, I thought.

Then the light turned green. Of course, not one of them looked to see if any cars were making left turns. But the nearest car was about five hundred yards away. I decided it was okay and let them walk.

I rubbed my head on every tree we passed. The mouse ears stuck like glue. By the time we got close to Main Street, we had been attacked by two Mexican bandits, three witches, a vampire, and some other thing. I don't know what the other thing was.

Arnie and Beth said they knew the vampire and both the Mexican bandits. The three witches called me by my name. They also smelled like melted plastic. I have no idea who they were. I just growled at *all* of them.

Then, when we got to the intersection of Maple Avenue and Main Street, there were four cars stopped there. Of course Arnie, Katie, Beth, and Mike thought they could cross. I knew better. It was my responsibility to knock them into a hedge.

Katie's cat tail came off. Her costume looked much better that way. The back of Beth's pumpkin got very flat, but she didn't know about it. Yet. Mike's costume looked just as rumpled as it had before. That was no problem. But one side of Arnie's face came off. I mean, the grease came off—not his face.

Arnie started to get mad. It was a good thing Mike told him he looked even more disgusting with half a face. Katie and I had to agree. Arnie calmed down.

We hadn't stopped at any houses yet. First we had to walk Katie to a Halloween party.

The Halloween party was a Saint Bernard's nightmare. All the doors were wide open. Kids—or whatever they were—were running in and out. There was no way anybody would know if there were any *real* burglars in there or not.

But it wasn't my problem. This wasn't my family. They may not have listened to me, anyway. The parents were clearly not too bright. It's a wonder humans get anything right. Not a day goes by when I'm not surprised by the things they decide to do.

But safe is safe. I decided I should check the place out before I let Katie go in there. After all, Katie belongs to me. I have to watch out for her no matter what.

I had a few minutes. She was still out in the yard trying to pin her tail back on.

It was a good thing I did, too. Right there on the table was a pile of food. The candy, the fruit, and the potato chips were fine. But right near the edge was a platter full of grilled hot dogs. With buns. They were definitely going to go bad.

I looked around. Nobody was watching. I stood on my hind legs and took care of the problem. No hot dogs, no stomachaches, I always say.

Happily, eating that sort of thing doesn't bother me a bit. I have a cast-iron stomach. It's a good thing my stomach is so strong. I have to eat a lot of food just to keep people from poisoning themselves! You can't be too careful.

I quietly slipped out the back door and around the side of the house. Katie had just gotten her tail back on. She looked just like those two cats, Sam and Janet. Awful.

She gave me a pat on the head and went into the party. Before I could count to two, Beth, Arnie, and Mike let out a whoop and disappeared past the gate.

Were they trying to lose me?

Maybe. They've tried it before. But they've always failed.

CHAPTER SIX

TAKE FROM THE RICH— AND EAT IT YOURSELF

The kids were two blocks ahead of me. But I caught up to them. I always get my kid. I'm like the Royal Canadian Mounted Police, who always get their man. Only I have more hair.

The kids still didn't smell right, but by this time I was used to it. I have a perfect memory for smells—even melted plastic mixed with Mounds and Milky Way bars, and Turkish Taffy.

There is something very strange about the idea of Halloween. I once read about how this strange custom started. It was in a copy of *Smithsonian* that wasn't bad. It was a bit too chewy. That's because they use such thick paper. Anyway, Halloween was weird then, and it still doesn't make any sense.

Halloween used to be called All Hallows' Eve. Humans thought that on one night of the year, all the souls of dead humans came back to earth and did anything they wanted.

They thought that meant the bad ones were going to come back and be bad.

The humans were so scared, they decided the only way to get these bad souls to behave was to give them snacks. That way, the bad souls would probably go over to someone else's house to be bad.

But, of course, none of this ever happened. It still doesn't. But did the humans forget about it? No. They let every kid out for the night dressed up like some kind of loony. The kids are supposed to go from door to door saying, "Trick or Treat."

This really means, "Give me candy, or I'll do something bad in your front yard."

Adult humans not only allow this, they think it's cute. Very strange.

But there is something even stranger that

happens on Halloween. They give the children all the candy they want on this night. Then, for the rest of the year, the adults get very upset at the children whenever they want to eat candy.

Does that whole story make sense?

Not to this dog.

Anyway, we went to every house in Big Bluff. We rang every doorbell. All the grownups came to the door and said, "Ooooh! How cute," no matter how disgusting the children looked.

Does this sound scared to you?

Most of the time, the kids don't even have time to say, "Trick or Treat." Buckets of candy appeared as soon as the doors opened. The kids dug into the buckets and filled their goody bags.

This wasn't the true spirit of Halloween. People should act a little bit scared. So I barked at other kids—just in case they really were mutant dwarfs from outer space. I also barked at all the grownups who came to the doors. I barked at everybody.

But did they get scared?

Nope. They said, "Hiya, Fred!"

I mean, where's the whole principle of All Hallows' Eve? No place in Big Bluff, let me tell you.

The whole time people were saying, "Hiya Fred," I was getting more and more embarrassed. People were laughing at me because of the mouse ears!

By the time we got to the last few houses, I couldn't stand it anymore. I stood out in the street. I watched cars go by. That made me even gloomier. When I was a puppy, I liked to chase cars. But I had to give it up. I have too much responsibility now. Every now and then I wish I could nibble at a few hubcaps again. Those were the good old days.

The best I can do is chase a few cats when everyone is out for the day. Or when the family is down with the flu. But that hardly ever happens. There are always one or two kids around to keep me from enjoying myself.

Finally I found a gate latch that looked like it might help me get those ears off. So I rubbed my head against the latch. The wire got stuck!

I yanked. I pulled. I lurched!

And the ears came loose.

But did they come off? Sort of.

The mouse ears came off the top of my head. But then they just swung down until they were hanging under my chin. This was not a help.

To make matters worse, Mike showed up at just that moment. He had his camera out in two seconds. He took my picture!

It was bad enough having to wear the stupid things. But to have Mike get a picture of me that would last forever—me, Fred the Fearless, the Houdini of Dogs—with mouse ears? It was unthinkable.

I vowed to get his camera. I would open it up, and destroy the film. But this would not be easy.

I knocked him into six bushes. He lost his goody bag for about half an hour. But I

39

found it for him. He also lost large sections of his bedding. He lost a shoe. But he didn't lose the camera.

I decided the next best thing to do was wait until he had the film developed. Then I would eat the pictures. There's more than one way to protect your good name, I always say.

Finally we were almost through with this insane trick-or-treating. The kids had about ten pounds of candy each. The mouse ears were still hanging under my chin, and there was only one house left—the old Griswold mansion!

CHAPTER SEVEN

A STICKY SITUATION

The old Griswold mansion would not be a problem. At least, that's what *I* thought. Boy, was I wrong.

You see, no one lived in the old Griswold mansion. Why Arnie, Beth, and Mike wanted to go there was beyond me. An empty house does not pop candy out the door and into your goody bag. But, as I've said before, I don't always understand people.

The kids said they wanted to go to the Griswold mansion because it looked haunted. You and I know there is no such thing as a ghost. Therefore, there is no such thing as a haunted house. But on Halloween,

41

people "suspend disbelief." That means you decide to believe anything—no matter how dumb. I read that in a newspaper once. I like that phrase.

Personally, I didn't care why they wanted to go to the Griswold mansion. All I knew was that the longest, worst night of the year was almost over. The kids would knock on the front door. Nobody would answer. Then we would all go home. I couldn't wait.

I was walking behind the group. Suddenly I stepped on something hard. It hurt. I lifted my foot and looked down. It was a piece of candy. I left it there and took another step. But then I stepped on another hard thing. That hurt, too. I was getting mad.

When I looked, it was another piece of candy. What was going on? Was it raining candy? I looked up. I saw nothing but tree branches and black sky. Then I heard small plopping noises. So I looked in front of me. There was a line of candy on the sidewalk.

I looked at Arnie. He was swinging his

goody bag. Pieces of candy were popping out of a hole in the bottom.

Good, I thought. Arnie would not be able to eat ten pounds of candy anyway. As I told you, Arnie is small.

I sniffed a piece. It smelled different, but it didn't smell too bad. Whatever it was, I had never tried that kind. Fudge, yes. Mints, of course. But this was weird. I decided it was time I tried something new.

Pieces of candy were dropping out of the goody bag at the rate of about one every three seconds. I was eating one of the strange new kind of candies every ten seconds. Of course, I spit out the wrappers. Soon I was chewing more and more slowly. Then suddenly it got *very* hard to chew.

I could barely open my mouth. In a few moments I could only open my lips. I had lockjaw!

I tried to stay calm. I blew my cheeks out a few times. Then I tried again. My jaw was cemented shut!

This candy was not good. In fact, it was

horrible stuff. I had eaten some of it, and now I was going to die! I would starve to death slowly. Painfully. Horribly. I moaned at the thought.

Facing death is very upsetting. I was so upset, I did a crazy thing. I promised that if I didn't die from this horrible experience, I would never chase another cat as long as I lived. That's how desperate I was.

Anyway, Arnie heard my moans. He stopped short. I moaned some more. Arnie turned around. Later, Arnie told everyone that I looked very strange. He said my eyes were rolling in my head, and I was crouched on the sidewalk waving my head back and forth.

I don't remember any of that. It didn't happen. He made up that whole story. Sometimes children add things onto stories to make them better.

Anyway, Arnie dropped his goody bag and came right to my side. He didn't even stop to pick up his candy pieces first. Arnie

has a kind heart. Then Beth and Mike came over, too. It took them a while to figure out the problem. Mike was the one who finally noticed the empty wrappers on the sidewalk.

"Turkish Taffy!" he said.

Beth picked up my lip. She looked at my teeth.

"Turkish Taffy," she said.

They sounded like a broken record.

Beth looked worried. She said, "If we don't get his teeth apart, he'll starve! Maybe we should *pull* them apart with a screwdriver!"

I moaned and backed up. It would be better to starve to death than have my teeth accidentally knocked in by a little girl with a screwdriver.

But Arnie said we didn't need a screwdriver. He said the Turkish Taffy would slowly melt away. That's because it is made of pure sugar.

Happily, Arnie was correct. As he said the words, I could already feel the disgusting stuff start to melt.

Then Arnie bent down and collected up all the candy pieces that were still lying on the sidewalk. He tied a knot in the bottom of his goody bag. By that time, the taffy had melted completely.

We started off, once again, toward the Griswold mansion.

But I was feeling grouchy. That crazy candy was dangerous stuff! I vowed that once we got home, I would take the goody bags. When the children were asleep, I would run down to the harbor and drop them off the end of the dock. If candy is bad for me, it *has* to be bad for them.

Suddenly I remembered my promise. I felt like an idiot. I had just promised never to chase cats again as long as I lived—if I lived. Now it looked as if I would live. What a mistake.

Next time, I thought, I will put a time limit on anything I promise. I'll say, "I promise not to chase cats for three whole months" or something. This is called a contract limitation. If you want to know the long word for it, it is part of the Rule Against Perpetuities.

I ate a law book once. It wasn't bad.

CHAPTER EIGHT

OUR ONLY FEAR WAS FEAR ITSELF

I was still feeling grouchy when we got to the Griswold mansion. It was broken down and creepy-looking. It used to be very elegant. Even fancy.

Though it is hard to believe, the Griswolds were rich people in the old days. But soon, only the two old Griswold sisters were living there. They had very little money. They didn't take care of the house. After they moved out, nobody else moved in. Basically, the house was a wreck.

I decided I should be the first to go up the front steps. After all, the porch might have rotten boards.

Once we got inside the gate, I ran ahead.

But Mike was right behind me. He had his camera ready. Beth and Arnie followed him. I stopped as soon as I got to the top step. Naturally, they all banged into me. They fell in a heap.

I got out from under them and listened carefully. There was a lot of noise when they all fell down. But I could have sworn I heard something else, too. I tried to listen. It was hard with all the whining and complaining.

Beth was complaining that her pumpkin was completely flat. It was true, but so what. Halloween was practically over. No one would see it anyway. Arnie said he banged his knee. Mike was worried about his camera. When he fell, he sat on it.

Personally, I hoped it was broken.

Then I heard the noise again.

Yes . . . there was definitely something fishy inside that house. Something was scrabbling around in there. Things are not supposed to scrabble around in empty houses.

I barked at the children to stay outside.

49

Then I threw myself at the door. I was planning to break it down.

It was a good plan, but the door was open. Instead of breaking down the door, I went flying into the house at about ninety miles an hour. This is not a good way to enter a dangerous building.

Naturally, the children didn't listen. Instead of waiting outside, they all came barreling in right behind me. They were too dumb to stay outside and wait for me to check it out first.

After all, there might be loose chandeliers. The chandeliers could come crashing down and flatten someone. There might be broken floorboards that would open up into big holes. All of them could fall right through the floor and into the cellar. Not only that, it was probably a fire hazard in there, too. These kids know nothing about safety.

They just stood there staring with their mouths open.

"I bet there's ghosts in here," whispered Beth.

Mike and Arnie's eyes looked big and bulgy—just like boiled eggs. It's not a great look.

I told them there is no such thing as ghosts, but they paid no attention. Sometimes I honestly think those children don't understand a word of Dog. *I* have no trouble with English. Why do they have so much trouble with Dog?

Maybe they just don't have an ear for languages.

It's true that there were sheets over all the furniture. There were lots of cobwebs hanging all over the place, too. But cobwebs don't mean ghosts. They mean spiders.

Then I heard the scrabbling noise again. I left the kids. I raced off to find out what was making the noise.

It could have been a burglar.

It could have been a prowler.

Even more important, it could have been someone who needed saving!

I checked the kitchen (no food). The pantry (very empty). The dining room (lots of broken chairs, broken mirrors, and a nasty-looking chandelier). And what must have been the library. There's no other reason to have all those books in one room. But why have a library in the house when you can just go down the street? I reminded myself to come back sometime during the day. There might be a few good books in there to eat.

There was no one in any of those rooms. There were no scrabbling noises either. So I kept searching.

I went back into the living room. Beth, Arnie, and Mike were standing there exactly the way I had left them. They looked as if they were made out of cement.

Good, I thought. Maybe they'll stay put for a change.

Suddenly I heard the scrabbling noise again. It was coming from the top of the stairs.

At this point I decided that extreme care was needed. Think about it. If someone needed rescuing, why would they just scrabble? Why wouldn't they call for help? It was quite possible that whatever was scrabbling up there was not good.

I started up the stairs as quietly as possible. After all, safe is safe.

I hadn't gone more than three steps when all three of the cement statues in the living room came to life. Of course, they started following me.

Two more steps, and then . . .

Screeee . . . ! My hair stood on end.

"What was that?" whispered Beth.

"A tree branch, scratching the window?" Mike said feebly.

Of course it was a tree branch. I knew that.

Four more steps, and then . . .

BANG!

"Don't shoot!" yelled Arnie.

All of us froze. But I quickly looked down. I saw that a gust of wind had blown the front door shut.

Phew! A nasty shock. But *I* wasn't scared. We kept climbing. Just as we got to the landing, I heard the scrabbling noise again. But this time it was close. Very close.

Then Beth screamed as a huge lump of yucky yellow stuff loomed around the corner. It started to attack!

"It's intergalactic slime!" yelled Mike.

CHAPTER NINE

INTERGALACTIC SLIME WOULD BE BETTER

Of course, at that point, Mike grabbed his camera. He was about to take a picture. Who cared about pictures at a time like that? I was in midleap. I had to save us from who knows what.

That thing could have zapped us with a ray gun. It could have had forty-five of its slimy, disgusting friends hiding in the bathroom.

But did Mike think of this? No. He whipped out his camera, and stepped right in front of me. My leap ended up being a plop. I knocked right into Mike and he dropped the camera. I tried to leap at that thing again.

Then it meowed.

Meow? I thought. Since when does intergalactic slime meow? I decided that just because it was intergalactic slime did not mean it was stupid. In fact, this particular slime might be making that noise to throw us off. It wanted to make us think it was harmless. It might be very clever intergalactic slime.

I was about to grab it and send it out the window when Beth knocked me flat on my face.

She raced over to the yellow slime, and pulled at it.

The yellow slime was a moldy blanket. Underneath was the sorriest excuse for a shivering black and white kitten I have ever seen in my life.

The kitten meowed again.

Beth scooped it up into her arms. She started making dumb cooing, drooling noises at it.

"It's a kitten," she crooned. "It's the cutest, sweetest, littlest honey-pie lamby-cat in the world!"

I didn't think it was cute. It wasn't sweet.

It was hardly a honey-pie. It didn't look like a lamb to me. It was just a small, ratty-looking cat. What was all the fuss about?

"See?" said Mike, looking right at me. "This house isn't haunted!"

Why look at me? I knew that all along. Mike was the one who yelled "intergalactic slime." Not me.

I was very disappointed.

My hope of saving the whole town—or even one person—was tossed right in the garbage. I would never make the front page of the *Big Bluff News* for finding a lost cat. Cats get lost all the time. When they get found, nobody thinks that's news. Least of all me.

What's more, if I had known it was a cat making that scrabbling noise, I *never* would have set foot in the Griswold mansion in the first place.

The whole night had been a disaster from the start. And I know this is hard to believe, but it was still going to get worse. Wait till I tell you what happened next.

Of course, the kids forgot all about Halloween. They rushed back home with the kitten. They were in such a hurry, they almost forgot their goody bags.

As we came up the walk, Katie was just getting home from her Halloween party.

"Look what we found!" Arnie said, pointing at the mangy little bundle in Beth's arms.

"Ooooh!" moaned Katie. "How cu-u-u-ute!"

Then Katie had to hold it. She had to pat it. She had to kiss it for about an hour. *Finally* they managed to get up the front steps and into the house.

Mr. and Mrs. Duff were sitting in the living room watching television.

"Can we keep it?" Katie and Arnie both whined together.

"Keep what?" Mr. and Mrs. Duff said together.

"Isn't it cu-u-u-ute?" said Kate. She held the kitten right under Mrs. Duff's nose.

"It certainly is," crooned Mrs. Duff. She reached out to hold the kitten.

Well, I won't go into *all* the boring and silly talk that took place that night. But Mr. Duff was on my side. He tried to tell Arnie and Katie that we didn't need another pet.

"Having Fred is like having seven or eight pets," said Mr. Duff.

I knew he meant I was *worth* seven or eight pets. I had to agree. I decided to forgive him for calling me a fathead after I saved his life. I could see he really appreciated me, even if he didn't always say so.

"We really don't need a kitten," said Mrs. Duff. "Fred is the most wonderful pet any family could have. . . . But it is awfully cute."

I really couldn't see what they were all so excited about.

But Katie and Arnie wouldn't stop begging and pleading. Mike and Beth were no help, either.

"I'd lo-o-o-ve to keep it," said Beth. "But my dad won't let me have cats. They might eat the frogs and snakes."

"I'd love to keep it," said Mike. "But my little brother is allergic to cats."

61

I'm allergic to cats, too. They make my teeth grind. But was anybody thinking of me? Nope.

After a whole lot of whining, the Duffs agreed to let the miserable cat stay.

I was ready to spit.

I have sacrificed everything for that family. How do they repay me? By bringing in yet another simpleminded little animal that needs to be watched every minute.

It was too much.

CHAPTER TEN

ANOTHER HOPELESS DUFF

Well, I don't have to tell you how the arrival of Fudge messed up everything. That's what they decided to call the kitten. Well, not exactly. You see, the kitten is black and white. It has a white nose, a white streak on its head, and white feet. They couldn't call him Blackie, and they couldn't call him Whitey, and they couldn't call him Boots. I figured they should just call him Hey You. Finally, after a whole bunch of arguing, they decided to call him Vanilla Fudge. But then they decided that was too long. So now they just call him Fudge for short.

Because of Fudge, they started messing up all the closets. Then the house was torn to shreds to make a bed for Fudge. They had to find a box. Not just *any* box. They had to find just the right box. Then they took a perfectly good blanket so he would be "warm and comfy."

Nobody ever goes to all that trouble to make a dog bed for *me*. Do they give *me* a box? Do they give *me* a blanket?

Next they took the whole thing and put it in the kitchen. That messed up the kitchen. They also had the nerve to put Fudge's bed right next to my food bowl.

After that, they warmed up some milk. They gave it to Fudge in a perfectly good cereal bowl. Fudge lapped up all the milk.

It was disgusting. How come nobody ever fixes *me* a bowl of warm milk before bed? Not that I would drink it, of course. But it is the thought that counts. Right?

When Fudge finished his milk, he started looking at my food bowl. I knew what *that* meant. I was about to chase him when I suddenly thought about my promise. Remem-

ber how I had promised never to chase cats
again?

I could have kicked myself. What a dumb
thing to have promised. Now I was stuck
with a cat who was actually living in the same
house with me. There was nothing I could
do about it! And that very cat was probably
going to eat everything in sight! Including
my food.

Well, I didn't exactly chase him. I went
over and stood nose to nose with him. But
did that scare Fudge? Nope.

He licked my nose!

Gross! I got kissed by a cat! It was horrible. His tongue was scratchy. He smelled
like warm milk! I hate warm milk almost as
much as I hate cats!

Not only that, everyone was watching!

"How adorable!" said Beth. She had a
goofy smile on her face.

"Isn't he a loving little thing!" said Mrs.
Duff. She had the same look.

"Hey, Fred," said Arnie. "He wants to be
your friend!"

Fat chance, I thought.

I quickly looked out the window. Getting kissed by a cat in front of your whole family is very bad. But it would be even worse if Winston, or Sam and Janet, happened to have seen that.

It was pitch-black outside. It was hard to tell if anyone was out there or not. I would never live it down if they were.

I scooted away from that cat as fast as I could go.

"Why don't you sleep in here with Fudge?" said Arnie. "That way he won't get lonely or scared."

No way, I thought. I'd rather sleep on an anthill.

Finally they got Fudge settled down in his bed. Then, at last, Arnie remembered to take the stupid mouse ears off me. They were still hanging down under my neck. Then they turned out the lights.

Soon everything was quiet. I lay down in the living room on the rug. I tried to think of a way to get rid of Fudge before morning.

I walked into the kitchen. Maybe if I pushed him out the dog door, he'd get lost. After all, he didn't know anything about this house yet. Maybe he'd end up at someone else's house. But first I had to wake him up. Maybe I could get him to go outside all by himself. Then it wouldn't really be my fault if he got lost.

But first I had to show him where the dog door was. On top of being sneaky, he struck me as pretty dumb, too. He'd never find it by himself.

As I got near his bed, he opened his eyes. He looked at me. He started purring.

"Don't get any ideas," I said gruffly. "And don't ever kiss me again."

Fudge smiled.

"And stay out of trouble," I said. "I have enough problems around here without having to worry about some simpleminded cat."

"I'll be good," he said. "Don't worry, Mommy."

My ears must have been playing tricks on me.

"My name is Fred," I said. "I'm *not* your mommy."

"Okay," said Fudge. "I love you, Mommy."

I rolled my eyes up to the ceiling. Clearly that cat was a born troublemaker.

"You want to see something interesting?" I said.

"Yes, Mommy," said Fudge.

I ignored the "Mommy" and walked over to my dog door.

"Just in case you want to take a little walk," I said, "this is what you do."

I pushed at the flap with my head. Fudge watched, but didn't move. I pushed further until the front half of me was outside.

It was so nice out there, I decided to get a breath of fresh air. So I went all the way out. Then I stuck my head back in and said, "You want to come?"

"Not now," said Fudge. "Maybe tomorrow."

Too bad. But there was still hope. I sat on the porch. Maybe he'd take a little walk later. Who knows.

Then I heard a noise like a clogged drain. It was on the front lawn. It could only be Winston.

"So I hear you have a new Duff over there," said Winston.

"Bad news travels fast," I answered.

After a short silence, Winston said, "It may not turn out to be so terrible."

I looked up at the moon. I tried to look on the bright side. Maybe he was right.

"Maybe the cat will run away," I said.

"That's true," said Winston. He made another gurgling noise. "If it doesn't, maybe it will spend most of its time out with Sam and Janet."

"I need to eat some grass," I finally said.

"Are you sick?" asked Winston.

"It must be nerves," I said.

Just then, Sam and Janet appeared on the lawn as if by magic. One minute those two are nowhere around. The next minute, they're right under your nose. I hate that.

"Lucky you," said Janet.

For once, they were not talking at the same time. I wondered what was going on.

"Maybe this new cat will teach you a thing or two," hissed Sam.

"Don't be silly," I said. I took a large mouthful of grass. My stomach felt as if little volcanoes were going off inside. "What could a kitten teach me?"

Sam and Janet smiled and started purring. I looked back at the house and got an awful sinking feeling. It was the purring that did it.

I knew that this was the worst day of my life—but only so far. It suddenly dawned on me that it was the beginning of the worst year of my life. Imagine me—Fred the Fearless, Fred the Houdini of Dogs and Protector of the Careless—having to take care of a cat. That is really scraping the bottom of the barrel.

"That kitten may teach you one of the most important things in life," Sam and Janet said together.

"And what would that be?" I asked. The hair on my back stood up.

"Love of cats!" they said.

Aaaarghhh!

THE END

or,

depending on how you look at it . . .

ONLY THE BEGINNING . . .